FLOWER·FAIRIES OF THE WAYSIDE

FLOWER·FAIRIES OF THE WAYSIDE

Poems and pictures by

CICELY MARY BARKER

FREDERICK WARNE

FREDERICK WARNE

Published by the Penguin Group
Penguin Books Ltd, 80 Strand, London WC2R 0RL, England
Penguin Putnam Inc., 375 Hudson Street, New York, N.Y. 10014, USA
Penguin Books Australia Ltd, 250 Camberwell Road, Camberwell,
Victoria 3124, Australia
Penguin Books Canada Ltd, 10 Alcorn Avenue, Toronto, Ontario, Canada M4V 3B2
Penguin Books (NZ) Ltd, Cnr Rosedale and Airborne Roads, Albany,
Auckland, New Zealand
Penguin Books India (P) Ltd, 11 Community Centre, Panchsheel Park,
New Delhi 110 017, India
Penguin Books (South Africa) (Pty) Ltd, PO Box 9, Parklands 2121, South Africa

Penguin Books Ltd, Registered Offices: 80 Strand, London WC2R 0RL, England

Web site at: www.flowerfairies.com

First published 1948
First published by Frederick Warne 1990
This edition first published 2002
1 3 5 7 9 10 8 6 4 2

ISBN 0 7232 4830 3

Printed in Hong Kong

CONTENTS

FOREWORD

I believe that many children would be glad to know how much of this book, and of the others in the Flower Fairy series, is true, and how much "pretend". So, let me say quite plainly, that I have drawn all the plants and flowers very carefully, from real ones; and everything that I have said about them is as true as I could make it. But I have never seen a fairy; the fairies and all about them are just "pretend". (It is nice to pretend about fairies.)

Now, I think, children will be able to tell the true parts from the pretend parts in these books.

I have gleaned from many sources my information about the flowers, their country names, and so on; but am especially indebted to the beautiful series of books "Wild Flowers as they Grow", by G. Clarke Nuttall (Cassell); and am grateful also for the help I have been given at Kew Gardens.

C.M.B

OPEN YOUR EYES!

To shop, and school, to work and play,
The busy people pass all day;
They hurry, hurry, to and fro,
And hardly notice as they go
The wayside flowers, known so well,
Whose names so few of them can tell.

They never think of fairy-folk
Who may be hiding for a joke!

O, if these people understood
What's to be found by field and wood;
What fairy secrets are made plain
By any footpath, road, or lane—
They'd go with open eyes, and *look*,
(As you will, when you've read this book)
And then at least they'd learn to see
How pretty common things can be!

The Jack-by-the-hedge Fairy

THE SONG OF
THE JACK-BY-THE-HEDGE FAIRY

"'Morning, Sir, and how-d'ye-do?
    'Morning, pretty lady!"
That is Jack saluting you,
    Where the lane is shady.

Don't you know him? Straight and tall—
    Taller than the nettles;
Large and light his leaves; and small
    Are his buds and petals.

Small and white, with petals four,
    See his flowers growing!
If you never knew before,
    There is Jack for knowing!

(Jack-by-the-hedge is also called Garlic Mustard, and Sauce Alone.)

THE SONG OF
THE GREATER CELANDINE FAIRY

You come with the Spring,
   O swallow on high!
You come with the Spring,
   And so do I.

Your nest, I know,
   Is under the eaves;
While far below
   Are my flowers and leaves.

Yet, to and fro
   As you dart and fly,
You swoop so low
   That you brush me by!

I come with the Spring;
   The wall is my home;
I come with the Spring
   When the swallows come.

(The name "Celandine" comes from the Greek word for "swallow",
and this celandine used sometimes to be called "swallow-wort".
It has orange-coloured juice in its stems, and is no relation to the
Lesser Celandine, from *Flower Fairies of the Spring*; but it is a relation
of the Horned Poppy, which you will find further on in this book.)

The Greater Celandine Fairy

The Ground Ivy Fairy

THE SONG OF
THE GROUND IVY FAIRY

In Spring he is found;
He creeps on the ground;
But someone's to blame
For the rest of his name—
For Ivy he's *not*!
Oh dear, what a lot
Of muddles we make!
It's quite a mistake,
And really a pity
Because he's so pretty;
He deserves a nice name—
Yes, *someone's* to blame!

(But he has some other names, which we do not hear very often;
here are four of them: Robin-run-up-the-dyke, Runnadyke,
Run-away-Jack, Creeping Charlie.)

THE SONG OF
THE RED CAMPION FAIRY

Here's a cheerful somebody,
　By the woodland's edge;
Campion the many-named,
　Robin-in-the-hedge.

Coming when the bluebells come,
　When they're gone, he stays,
(Round Robin, Red Robin)
　All the summer days.

Soldiers' Buttons, Robin Flower,
　In the lane or wood;
Robin Redbreast, Red Jack,
　Yes, and Robin Hood!

The Red Campion Fairy

The Rose-Bay Willow-Herb Fairy

THE SONG OF
THE ROSE-BAY
WILLOW-HERB FAIRY

On the breeze my fluff is blown;
So my airy seeds are sown.

Where the earth is burnt and sad,
I will come to make it glad.

All forlorn and ruined places,
All neglected empty spaces,

I can cover—only think!—
With a mass of rosy pink.

Burst then, seed-pods; breezes, blow!
Far and wide my seeds shall go!

(Another name for this Willow-Herb is "Fireweed", because of its
way of growing where there have been heath or forest fires.)

THE SONG OF
THE BLACK MEDICK FAIRIES

"Why are we called 'Black', sister,
    When we've yellow flowers?"
"I will show you why, brother:
    See these seeds of ours?
Very soon each tiny seed
    Will be turning black indeed!"

The Black Medick Fairies

The Bee Orchis Fairy

THE SONG OF
THE BEE ORCHIS FAIRY

In the grass o' the bank,
   by the side o' the way,
      Where your feet may stray
      On your luckiest day,
There's a sight most rare
   that your eyes may see:
A beautiful orchis that looks like a bee!
A velvety bee, with a proud little elf,
Who looks like the wonderful
   orchis himself—
      In the grass o' the hill,
      Not often, but still
      Just once in a way
      On your luckiest day!

THE SONG OF
THE WHITE BINDWEED FAIRY

O long long stems that twine!
O buds, so neatly furled!
O great white bells of mine,
(None purer in the world)
Each lasting but one day!
O leafy garlands, hung
In wreaths beside the way—
Well may your praise be sung!

(But this Bindweed, which is a big sister to the little pink
Field Convolvulus, is not good to have in gardens, though it
is so beautiful; because it winds around other plants and trees.
One of its names is "Hedge Strangler". Morning Glories are
a garden kind of Convolvulus.)

The White Bindweed Fairy

The Red Clover Fairy

THE SONG OF
THE RED CLOVER FAIRY

The Fairy: O, what a great big bee
Has come to visit me!
He's come to find my honey.
O, what a great big bee!

The Bee: O, what a great big Clover!
I'll search it well, all over,
And gather all its honey.
O, what a great big Clover!

THE SONG OF
THE SELF-HEAL FAIRY

When little elves have cut themselves,
    Or Mouse has hurt her tail,
Or Froggie's arm has come to harm,
    This herb will never fail.
The Fairy's skill can cure each ill
    And soothe the sorest pain;
She'll bathe, and bind, and soon they'll find
    That they are well again.

(This plant was a famous herb of healing in old days,
as you can tell by the names it was given—Self-Heal,
All-Heal, and others. It is also called Prunella.)

The Self-Heal Fairy

The Stork's-Bill Fairy

THE SONG OF
THE STORK'S-BILL FAIRY

"Good morning, Mr Grasshopper!
    Please stay and talk a bit!"
"Why yes, you pretty Fairy;
    Upon this grass I'll sit.
And let us ask some riddles;
    They're better fun than chat:
Why am I like the Stork's-bill?
    Come, can you answer that?"

"Oh no, you clever Grasshopper!
    I fear I am a dunce;
I cannot guess the answer—
    I give it up at once!"
"When children think they've caught me,
    I'm gone, with leap and hop;
And when they gather Stork's-bill,
    Why, all the petals drop!"

(The Stork's-bill gets her name from the long seed-pod, which looks
like a stork's beak or bill. Others of her family are called Crane's-bills.)

THE SONG OF
THE SOW THISTLE FAIRY

I have handsome leaves, and my stalk is tall,
   And my flowers are prettily yellow;
Yet nobody thinks me nice at all:
   They think me a tiresome fellow—
      An ugly weed
      And a rogue indeed;
For wherever I happen to spy,
     As I look around,
     That they've dug their ground,
I say to my seeds "Go, fly!"

    And because I am found
    On the nice soft ground,
    A trespassing weed am I!

(But I have heard that Sow Thistle is good rabbit-food,
so perhaps it is not so useless as most people think.)

The Sow Thistle Fairy

The Tansy Fairy

THE SONG OF
THE TANSY FAIRY

In busy kitchens, in olden days,
Tansy was used in a score of ways;
Chopped and pounded,
   when cooks would make
Tansy puddings and tansy cake,
Tansy posset, or tansy tea;
Physic or flavouring tansy'd be.
       People who know
       Have told me so!

That is my tale of the past; today,
Still I'm here by the King's Highway,
Where the air from the fields
   is fresh and sweet,
With my fine-cut leaves and my flowers neat.
Were ever such button-like flowers seen—
Yellow, for elfin coats of green?
       Three in a row—
       I stitch them so!

THE SONG OF
THE RIBWORT PLANTAIN FAIRY

Hullo, Snailey-O!
How's the world with *you*?
Put your little horns out;
Tell me how you do?
There's rain, and dust, and sunshine,
Where carts go creaking by;
You like it wet, Snailey;
I like it dry!

Hey ho, Snailey-O,
I'll whistle you a tune!
I'm merry in September
As e'er I am in June.
By any stony roadside
Wherever you may roam,
All the summer through, Snailey,
Plantain's at home!

(There are some other kinds of Plantain besides this.
The one with wide leaves, and tall spikes of seed which
canaries enjoy, is Greater Plantain.)

The Ribwort Plantain Fairy

The Fumitory Fairy

THE SONG OF
THE FUMITORY FAIRY

Given me hundreds of years ago,
My name has a meaning you shall know:
It means, in the speech of the bygone folk,
"Smoke of the Earth" —a soft green smoke!

A wonderful plant to them I seemed;
Strange indeed were the dreams they dreamed,
Partly fancy and partly true,
About "Fumiter" and the way it grew.

Where men have ploughed
    or have dug the ground,
Still, with my rosy flowers, I'm found;
Known and prized by the bygone folk
As "Smoke of the Earth" —
    a soft green smoke!

(The name "Fumitory" was "Fumiter" 300 years ago; and long before
that, "Fume Terre", which is the French name, still, for the plant.
"Fume" means "smoke", "terre" means "earth".)

THE SONG OF
THE HORNED POPPY FAIRY

These are the things I love and know:
The sound of the waves, the sight of the sea;
The great wide shore when the tide is low;
Where there's salt in the air, it's home to me—
With my petals of gold—the home for me!

The waves come up and cover the sand,
Then turn at the pebbly slope of the beach;
I feel the spray of them, where I stand,
Safe and happy, beyond their reach—
With my marvellous horns—
 beyond their reach!

The Horned Poppy Fairy

The Chicory Fairy

THE SONG OF
THE CHICORY FAIRY

By the white cart-road,
  Dusty and dry,
Look! there is Chicory,
  Blue as the sky!

Or, where the footpath
  Goes through the corn,
See her bright flowers,
  Each one new-born!

Though they fade quickly,
  O, have no sorrow!
There will be others
  New-born tomorrow!

(Chicory is also called Succory.)

THE SONG OF
THE JACK-GO-TO-BED-
AT-NOON FAIRY

I'll be asleep by noon!
Though bedtime comes so soon,
  I'm busy too.
Twelve puffs!—and then from sight
I shut my flowers tight;
Only by morning light
  They're seen by you.

Then, on some day of sun,
They'll open wide, each one,
  As something new!
Shepherd, who minds his flock,
Calls it a Shepherd's Clock,
Though it can't say "tick-tock"
  As others do!

(Another of Jack's names, besides Shepherd's Clock is Goat's Beard.)

The Jack-go-to-bed-at-noon Fairy

The Agrimony Fairies

THE SONG OF
THE AGRIMONY FAIRIES

Spikes of yellow flowers,
    All along the lane;
When the petals vanish,
    Burrs of red remain.

First the spike of flowers,
    Then the spike of burrs;
Carry them like soldiers,
    Smartly, little sirs!

Also by Cicely Mary Barker

Flower Fairies of the Spring
Flower Fairies of the Summer
Flower Fairies of the Autumn
Flower Fairies of the Winter
Flower Fairies of the Trees
Flower Fairies of the Garden
A Flower Fairy Alphabet